All Afloat on Noah's Boat!

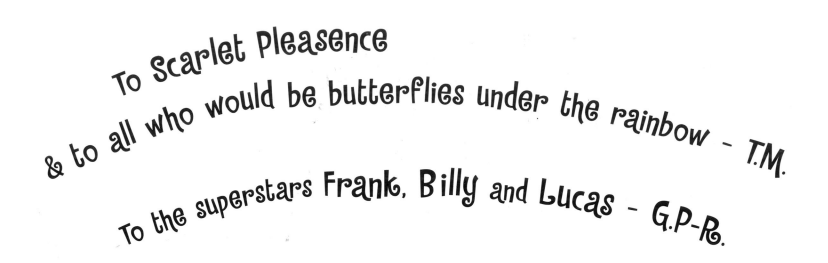

To Scarlet Pleasence
& to all who would be butterflies under the rainbow – T.M.

To the superstars Frank, Billy and Lucas – G.P-R.

ORCHARD BOOKS
338 Euston Road, London NW1 3BH
Orchard Books Australia
Level 17/207 Kent Street, Sydney, NSW 2000

ISBN 978 1 84616 242 8

First published in 2006 by Orchard Books
First published in paperback in 2007

Text © Tony Mitton 2006
Illustrations © Guy Parker-Rees 2006

The rights of Tony Mitton to be identified as the author
and of Guy Parker-Rees to be identified as the illustrator
of this work have been asserted by them in accordance
with the Copyright, Designs and Patents Act, 1988.

A CIP catalogue record for this book is available from the British Library.

12 14 16 18 20 19 17 15 13

Printed in China

Orchard Books is a division of Hachette Children's Books,
an Hachette UK company.
www.hachette.co.uk

All Afloat on Noah's Boat!

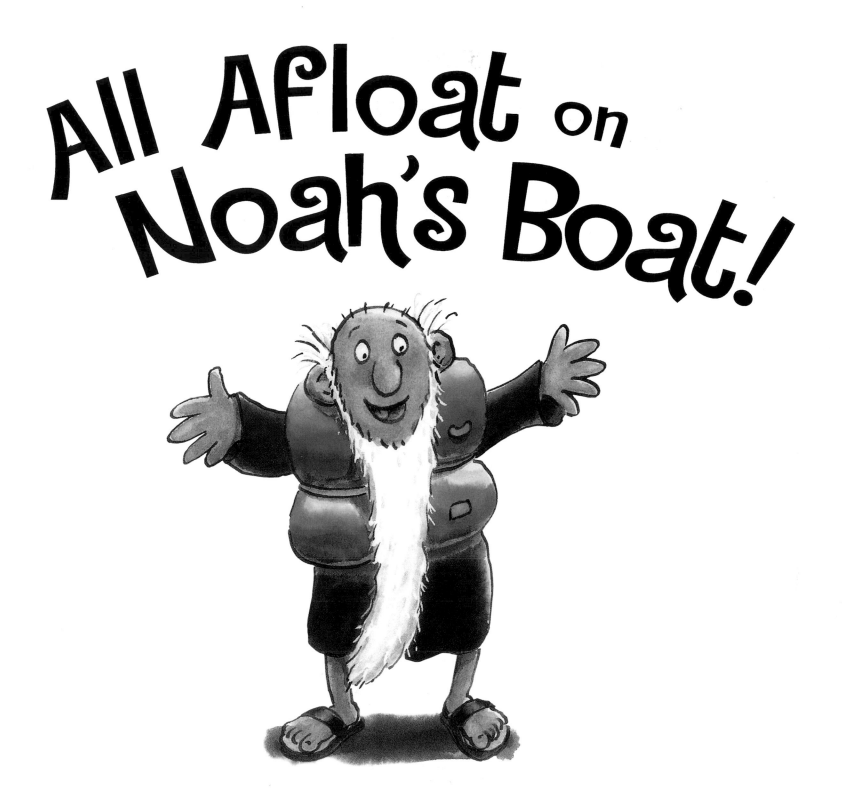

Tony Mitton ◆ Guy Parker-Rees

ORCHARD

Bang bang, tap tap, chip chip chip.
Noah built a house in the shape of a ship.
He built it wide and he built it tall.
He built it for creatures great and small.

When the rain came down, Noah clanged his bell,
crying, "All aboard the Ark Hotel!
The ground's getting wet. It'll soon be mud.
Come and keep safe
from the rising flood."

So, along came the creatures, all in pairs,
flying through the windows, stepping up the stairs,
filling up the Ark with a racket and a row.
There were snakes in the stern
and bears in the bow.

The rain rattled down on the **great big boat,**

till the water rose and made it float.

All they could see was flood and sky, but aboard Noah's Ark they were safe and dry.

Well, the **days** went by
and the **weeks** went past,

and it seemed that the flood
would last and last.

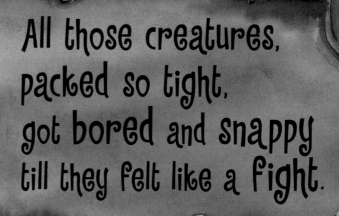

All those creatures,
packed so tight,
got bored and snappy
till they felt like a fight.

The lions and the leopards turned mean and catty.

And, **boy**, those rodents sure were **ratty!**

There were animal **tantrums**

and insect **tiffs**,

and the birds **nearly** came to feathery **biffs**.

So, Noah stood up, saying,
"Hush and hark!
Any more fuss and you're off my Ark!

The rain's stopped falling,
but the flood's not done,
So, while we're here, let's have some fun.
We'll all get ready for a Talent Show.
You can all do SOMETHING, isn't that so?"

Clever old Noah
That did the trick.
There were no more quarrels
or fights to pick.

When at last it was time
to begin the show,
old Noah said, "Well?
Are you ready?

So, the animals came on
two by two,
to show the things
that they could do.

GO!"

The frogs sprang on doing hyper-hops.

They flipped all over the table tops.

The toucans played a **rhythmic** peck,
with **tapping** beaks, upon the deck.

But nobody heard
the **caterpillars** croon,

"We're wrapping ourselves
in a tight cocoon."

The snakes both **tied** themselves in **knots**.

The leopards **wiggled** all their **spots**.

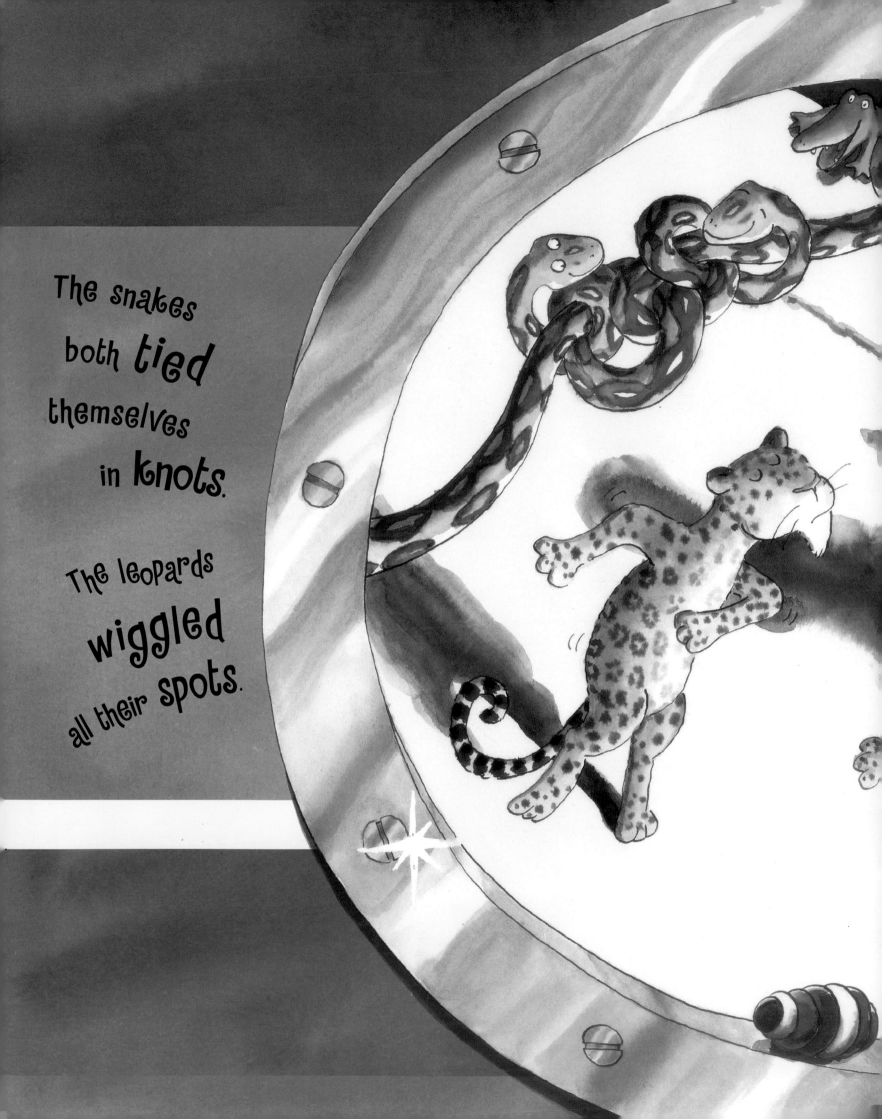

Oh, what a
rumpus!

Oh, what a
row!

That Talent Show
got **busy** now!

But the poor little caterpillars
lay quite still,
all wrapped up on the windowsill.

The crocodiles balanced on the tips of their tails.

The monkeys screeched out mega-wails.

The Talent show
was such a ball,
there's not the space
to tell it all.

And the caterpillars thought,
"They're all so good.
We'd both join in
if we only could."

But when the show was nearly through,
Noah whispered, "One more act to do . . . . "

Each caterpillar's tight cocoon
looked like it might crack open soon . . .

They'd both turned into **butterflies!**

They spread their brilliant wings out wide
and every single creature sighed.

"They're **beautiful!**" said Noah. "**Oh, my!**
They've opened up their wings to fly.
But look – out there the water's **gone!**
That means there's **land** to live upon."

"The butterflies can end our show.

Let's wave goodbye and watch them go . . . "

Then the creatures came out, two by two,
on a world that waited, bright and new.